DARRYL THE DINOSAUR

Dedicated to Max
I had no idea what happiness
truly was until I saw your
smile

There's a store where all the Stuffys live.

STUFFYS

A big store with Stuffys as far as you can see.

All the boys and girls come to this store to find their stuffy.

Big Stuffys, Small Stuffys, Round Stuffys, Tall Stuffys

Stuffys that fly

and Stuffys that swim

But there was one Stuffy the boys and girls would not take home....

A DINOSAUR!!

When a child would pick him up they always put him back down.

"Why not me?" he'd ask with a frown.

The answer was always the same, "He's Broken!"

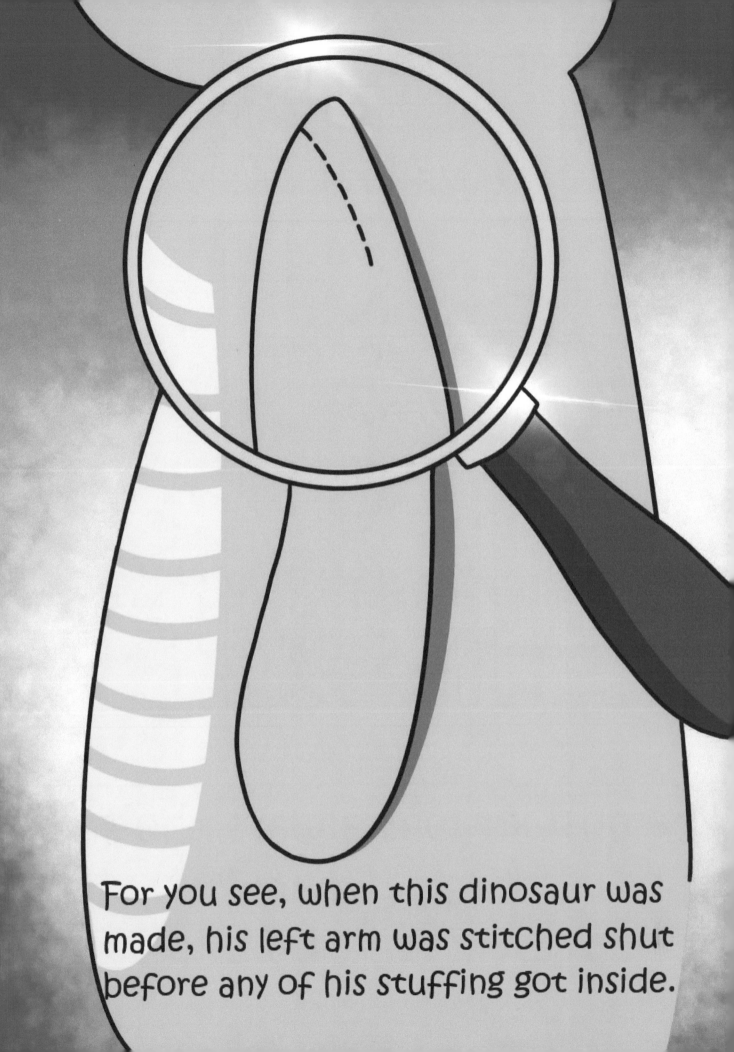

For you see, when this dinosaur was made, his left arm was stitched shut before any of his stuffing got inside.

His left arm is thin and flat.
Not full and strong like his right arm.

Time after time, the dinosaur watched as his friends found their kids and their new homes.

The children's eyes would light up when they found their Stuffy, and the Stuffys would smile knowing they were going to be loved.

One day a boy came in and searched
through all the Stuffys.

"Find the perfect one!", his mom said.

After searching the store, the boy
found the dinosaur and reached out
to pick him up.

The dinosaur waited again to hear...
...that he was broken...

"He's special like me!", the boy shouted

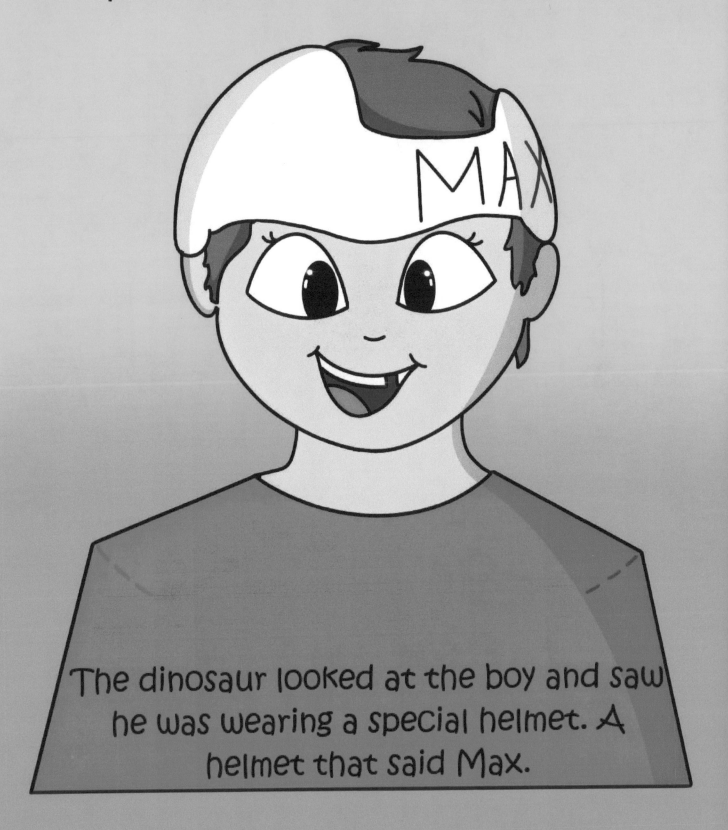

The dinosaur looked at the boy and saw he was wearing a special helmet. A helmet that said Max.

"Hi! I'm Max!" he told the dinosaur "Do you want to come home with me?"

Max squeezed the dinosaur and the dinosaur squeezed back.

"What is his name?" Mom asked.
"Darryl", said Max
"Darryl the Dinosaur"
"We're going to have so many adventures together!"

And did they ever...

Be on the lookout for future adventures of
Darryl & Max™
online and at your local bookstore

For updates on Darryl the Dinosaur™
and all things Darryl & Max™
Follow us on Instagram @darrylthedinosaur
and on Facebook Darryl the Dinosaur

About Us

Justin Mendez grew up in the suburbs of Chicago. He has a love for making up and telling stories. He now resides in Wisconsin with his wife and son who inspired him to put pen to paper.

Payton Weirich lives in Wisconsin and is 14 years old. One of Payton's favorite hobbies is to draw. She loves art in all of its shapes and forms. Payton is currently in 8th grade and ready for a full life's work ahead of her.

CPSIA information can be obtained
at www.ICGtesting.com
Printed in the USA
LVHW071528220123
737718LV00015B/106